THE ELIZABETH

KRIS BALLARD

THE ELIZABETH
Copyright © 2020 by Kris Ballard

All rights reserved. This book or any portion thereof may not be reproduced or used in any manner whatsoever without the express written permission of the publisher except for the use of brief quotations in a book review.

ISBN: 978-1-7333425-2-0

TABLE OF CONTENTS

Dedication 5

Section I: Margaret Fuller 7
   Chapter 1: Precocious Daughter 9
   Chapter 2: The Dial 15
   Chapter 3: New York City 21
   Chapter 4: Revolution 27
   Chapter 5: The Pope 33
   Chapter 6: Courage 39
   Chapter 7: Marble 45
   Chapter 8: Family and Friends 51

Section II: The Elizabeth 57
   Chapter 9: Shipwrecked 59
   Chapter 10: The Wreckers 65
   Chapter 11: Memoirs 71
   Chapter 12: The Secret Six 77
   Chapter 13: War 83
   Chapter 14: Horace Greeley 91
   Chapter 15: Julia Ward Howe 99
   Chapter 16: Legacy 107

DEDICATION

This book is dedicated to my daughter, Samantha Elizabeth Ballard. My hope is that she will be inspired by the example of Margaret Fuller.

SECTION I
MARGARET FULLER

CHAPTER 1
PRECOCIOUS DAUGHTER

There was once a very precocious little girl. Her father was a politician whom she loved more than life itself. However, sometimes her dad could be a bit demanding. This little girl's name was Margaret Fuller, and she lived in Massachusetts. Actually, her full name was Sarah Margaret Fuller, but she insisted on being called Margaret.

Margaret Fuller was born in the year 1810 and, by the time she was three and a half, she knew how to read and write. Young Margaret experienced tragedy when her fourteen-month-old sister, Julia Adelaide, died.

Margaret's mother was also named Margaret. She loved her mother, but it was her father who supervised her education. Most parents were happy if their children learned their ABCs by the time they were three and a half. However, Margaret's father Timothy expected a great deal more.

On one hand, it was great for a young girl to have someone who was deeply interested in her education. On the other hand, being pushed to learn so much was overwhelming. Margaret's dad was a lawyer and a Harvard graduate. Before Timothy Fuller got involved in politics, he worked as a school teacher. So at a very young age, his daughter Margaret was being taught by a scholar.

Indeed, every evening Margaret was required to explain to her dad what she had learned that day. Her father didn't accept excuses, so Margaret did her best to meet his unrealistic expectations. At that time, many American intellectuals were Unitarians, a very progressive form of Christianity.

As the oldest child, Margaret was expected to help her mother with household chores in addition to studying. Although the death of her sister Julia had been tragic, Margaret soon had a little brother named Eugene. He was five years younger than Margaret, and she helped care for him.

When she was six years old, Margaret was already studying Latin as well as many other difficult subjects. She studied with poor lighting, which damaged her eyesight and forced her to wear glasses. Margaret always wanted her father's approval, so she continued with her studies.

The year 1817 was an eventful year for the Fuller family. This was the year Timothy Fuller was elected to Congress. This was also the year Margaret's brother, William Fuller, was born. Now Margaret had two brothers.

When Congress was in session, Margaret's dad wasn't able to supervise her education. Although her father's teaching methods had traumatized her, he had succeeded in producing a genius. However, Margaret had no social skills so it was quite a shock for her when she was enrolled in the Port School when she was nine years old.

Margaret had never attended a regular school. What a horrible experience! The other girls were snobs and she felt so awkward trying to socialize with them. Of course, her classmates thought she was the snob and they hated her for her book learning. They didn't mean to bully her, but they couldn't help it since she was such an easy target.

Margaret obviously wasn't going to receive a rigorous education at the Port School. However, she did begin to learn how to interact with children who were her own age. Margaret didn't like being forced to attend school, but she tried her best to adapt to it.

The Port School was actually a school for boys who planned to attend Harvard. Though girls were allowed to attend the Port School, the chances of Margaret ever being able to attend Harvard was very slim. Not because she wasn't smart enough, but because women weren't allowed to attend that college. In fact, women weren't allowed to attend any college in America. This certainly didn't seem fair to Margaret, especially since her father had graduated from Harvard.

Although Margaret's father had been a tough taskmaster, she missed him when he was serving in Congress. She wrote lengthy letters to him and was proud that he was an accomplished politician. Then one day, Margaret overheard a conversation between her parents. Her mother said, "I worry that our daughter will never get married." Her father replied, "Why does Margaret need to get married? She is only ten years old."

The Elizabeth

Her mother countered, "You know what I mean. Our daughter is smart, but she doesn't know how to talk to people." Her father agreed, saying, "That's true. She does have a few rough edges. I think Margaret needs to continue attending a regular school so she can learn how to socialize with the other children."

Margaret's heart sank! She wanted to burst into the room and tell her parents they were wrong. But, she didn't do that, because she knew eavesdropping was wrong. So Margaret kept her knowledge of this conversation to herself.

Margaret hated school, not because school was difficult, but rather, because it was too easy. She also hated how the other children stared at her because she wore glasses. Although Margaret wasn't happy about attending school, there was nothing she could do about it.

It hurt Margaret when her mother said that she might never get married. Although she couldn't picture herself as a married woman, she still hoped to be happily married someday. So Margaret continued attending school, as well as being tutored by her father when he wasn't in Washington DC.

When Margaret Fuller was fourteen years old, something unusual happened. Her father decided not to run for re-election to Congress. He had served for eight years, but now he wanted to spend his time working on a Presidential Campaign.

So Timothy Fuller helped John Quincy Adams become President of the United States. This was good, but now

Margaret's father was no longer a member of Congress. Although her father was still sharp as a tack, he no longer had the prestige of serving in Congress.

At this awkward time in her father's career, Margaret finally found a best friend. Her friend was named Lydia, but everybody called her Maria. Lydia Maria Francis was eight years older than Margaret.

Maria was a school teacher in Watertown, Massachusetts. Even more impressive than that, Maria had written and published a novel called *Hobomok*. The book was way ahead of its time.

One of the main characters was a Native American named Hobomok. Maria was one of the first American authors who actually showed any respect for Native Americans. Margaret and Maria were both scholars who enjoyed studying together. For the first time in Margaret's life, she no longer felt lonely. It felt good to have someone who understood her.

At this time, Margaret also began to make friends with some young men. She was close friends with Jameson Fisher. Margaret liked Jameson because he pretended to be a feminist. Of course, he was only doing this in order to impress her.

Margaret also was jealous of Jameson because he was a student at Harvard. It wasn't fair that he was able to attend Harvard when she couldn't. Margaret believed that some-

The Elizabeth

day women would be allowed to attend Harvard, though she didn't think it was going to happen soon enough to help her.

She may have been a feminist, but that didn't mean that she wasn't attracted to men. If a young man attended Harvard and was also a Unitarian, then she was probably friends with him. Since Margaret was raised a Unitarian, she felt very comfortable with people of her own faith. There weren't very many Unitarians in America, but some Unitarians were very influential at Harvard.

In 1833, Margaret's father decided to move the entire family to Groton, Massachusetts. Groton was forty miles from Boston. Timothy Fuller may have been an intelligent man, but Margaret thought this was the dumbest idea her father ever had.

Margaret felt so isolated in Groton. She was 23 years old and beginning to think her mother had been right when she said Margaret might never get married. Margaret wasn't happy, but she decided to make the best of a bad situation. She began to write. Although Margaret had always been a good writer, now she began to take her writing seriously.

CHAPTER 2
THE DIAL

Timothy Fuller didn't really want to live in Groton either. Why had he moved the family there? He had run out of money. Margaret's father was a lawyer and his business had failed. So he did the best he could for his family by moving them to a farm in Groton.

Then one day in 1835, Margaret Fuller became terribly ill. She had often been sickly, but this time she was so sick it frightened her. While Margaret was trying to recover from her illness, her father died from cholera.

Timothy Fuller may not have been perfect, but he meant everything to Margaret. So she put her personal plans of traveling to Europe on hold and told her mother she would take responsibility for the family. This was certainly a time when Margaret wished she was a man.

Unfortunately, Margaret's father hadn't left a will, so her uncles took control of her family's money. Since her uncles were greedy, they wouldn't let Margaret or her family have very much money.

Although Margaret's parents had eight children, only six of them were still living. Margaret wasn't sure how she was

The Elizabeth

going to help her family, but she did know that she wasn't going to stay in Groton. Soon Margaret found a job as a school teacher in Boston. Things were different in Boston now. Her old friend Jameson Fisher had married a socialite and moved to New York City. Also some of her other friends had moved away.

However, working as a school teacher was a great opportunity. Margaret was happy to work for Bronson Alcott at the Temple School. Alcott reminded Margaret of her dad. He didn't have much money, yet he was still highly influential.

The Temple school was controversial because Alcott used progressive teaching methods. He also had some ideas about the Bible that many people thought were offensive. Originally, the Temple School had thirty students, but parents began removing their children.

Although Margaret enjoyed teaching at this school, she soon realized that the school wasn't making any money. Though Margaret admired Alcott, she knew that she needed to find a different job. So she went to teach in Providence, Rhode Island.

The Greene Street School paid Margaret $1,000 dollars a year. This was more money than she ever thought she would make. Hiram Fuller was in charge of this school. Although they weren't related, Margaret and Hiram worked well together.

Eventually the family farm in Groton was sold, with Margaret and the Fuller family moving to Jamaica Plain, Massachusetts. She was delighted to be living in the Boston area again. For Margaret, Boston always felt like home.

When Margaret was living in Jamaica Plain, she began holding conversations. These conversations weren't idle chit-chat, but rather an intellectual salon for women. Margaret was now 29 years old and felt that women needed the same intellectual opportunities as men.

The conversations were well-attended and the participants felt like they were learning a lot. Thirty women attended the first conversation, so Margaret decided to continue having these get-togethers.

At this time, Ralph Waldo Emerson asked Margaret to be the editor of *The Dial*. Margaret was close friends with Emerson, so she accepted this position. The Dial was a magazine about transcendentalism, a popular philosophy with many Boston intellectuals. Margaret considered herself a transcendentalist, but she also valued her Unitarian faith. However, some transcendentalists were opposed to Unitarianism.

So Margaret began editing *The Dial* in 1840. It was great experience because she got to hobnob with a lot of her intellectual friends. For instance, her former employer, Bronson Alcott was an influential transcendentalist.

Then, of course, there was Ralph Waldo Emerson. For several years, Margaret had been friends with Emerson and his

The Elizabeth

wife. She thought Emerson was a fascinating man. Emerson was seven years older than Margaret and he was a graduate of Harvard Divinity School.

However, Ralph Waldo Emerson had lost his faith in traditional Christianity after the death of his first wife in 1831. He had only been married for two years when his wife died from tuberculosis. After her death, Emerson questioned everything. Since nothing seemed to make sense anymore, Emerson toured Europe in 1833.

While Emerson was in Europe, he had the opportunity to meet many famous intellectuals. He even became close friends with Thomas Carlyle. In 1835, Emerson got married again. His new wife Lydia was an intellectual, but he called her Lidian. It was a play on words, but his wife went along with it.

Then, in 1838, Emerson was asked to give an important speech at Harvard Divinity School. He shocked many people with the things he said. Emerson's Christian beliefs were so unorthodox that some people thought he was an atheist.

Although Emerson was popular on the lecture circuit, he wasn't going to be asked to speak again at Harvard Divinity School anytime soon. This was ironic, since Emerson was a graduate of that school.

Margaret was in the audience when Emerson delivered his controversial speech. She admired Emerson and he had a great deal of respect for her. Margaret always enjoyed speaking with Emerson, because he was a deep thinker and he treated her fairly.

Editing *The Dial* was more difficult than Margaret thought it would be. Since nearly everyone who wrote for *The Dial* was a dreamer, they were constantly getting sidetracked by impractical ideas.

Margaret was supposed to be paid $200 per year for editing the magazine, but hadn't received any money for her work. *The Dial* had such a small readership that there wasn't even enough money to pay for the printing expenses. Clearly, *The Dial* wouldn't be able to continue if it was not making money.

Although Margaret Fuller was the editor of *The Dial*, George Ripley was the managing editor. Out of all the Transcendentalists, Ripley was the biggest dreamer of them all. Margaret could still remember the day Ripley told everyone he was forming a commune.

George Ripley and his wife intended to buy a 170-acre farm. They planned to finance the purchase of the farm by getting other people to help them pay for it. Soon there was enough money. They purchased the land and started a commune named Brook Farm. People began to move there, but Margaret had no desire to live there.

She already had her fill of farming when she lived in Groton. Although Margaret never invested in Brook Farm, she still ended up becoming an honorary member of the commune.

The Elizabeth

Frequent visits to Brook Farm were more than enough for Margaret. Though many of her friends lived there, Margaret preferred living in the big city.

Margaret edited *The Dial* for two years, but never received pay for the work she did. So she set up a private meeting with Emerson. Margaret valued his friendship and didn't want to say anything she would regret. Margaret had her father's temper, which she hoped wouldn't surface when she met with Emerson.

At the meeting Margaret said, "I have edited *The Dial* for two years and I have never been paid for my work. If you want me to continue working, then you need to pay me." Emerson replied, "You have been very patient. I must admit that this magazine has been a financial flop. I don't blame you for no longer wanting to edit it."

Margaret responded, "I am not going to ask for the $400 I am owed, because I thoroughly enjoyed the work. However, I am now going to spend my time getting paid what I'm worth." Emerson gave Margaret a big hug and said, "Several years ago when I first met you, I didn't think I was going to like you."

He continued, "I unfairly judged you. Now I realize what a noble heart you have." Margaret blushed and thought, "How can I ever be angry with Emerson when he always knows the right things to say?" Now, editing *The Dial* would be Emerson's responsibility. Margaret knew with her heart and her intellect that he would have just as much trouble editing the magazine as she had experienced.

CHAPTER 3
NEW YORK CITY

In the summer of 1843, Margaret Fuller decided to do some traveling. Her journey took her through the Great Lakes region. She visited the small town of Chicago and even went to Mackinac Island. Since Margaret was a bit of a homebody, it felt great to travel around seeing new things and new places.

Margaret was now 33 years old and an important intellectual. Not only did she want to travel, but she also wanted to write a book about her visit to the Great Lakes. She had never written a book before, but she was looking forward to the challenge.

What she enjoyed most about the Great Lakes was visiting with Native Americans. She had a genuine respect for them, which was unusual in those days. Indeed, many people thought it was odd that she had any concern at all for the Indians.

When Margaret returned home, she wanted to do some research before she wrote her book. So she got special permission to use the Harvard Library. Margaret Fuller was the first woman who had ever been allowed to use that library. Although it was an honor to do her research there, she still was bitter that women weren't allowed to attend Harvard.

When Margaret felt that she had done enough research, she began to write her book. In 1844, Margaret finished writing *Summer on the Lakes, in 1843*. Margaret was proud of the book she had written, and it was well-received.

Margaret Fuller had to admit that it felt great to be a published author. The same year her book was published, she accepted a job offer from the *New York Tribune*. Horace Greeley, the man in charge of the *Tribune*, agreed to pay Margaret $500 dollars a year to be a literary critic.

Many people read the *Tribune*, so Margaret knew she would be paid for her work. This was an awesome feeling and Margaret was happy that she'd be working for Greeley. He was slightly older than Margaret and had started working in the newspaper industry when he was a teenager, before starting the *New York Tribune* in 1841.

Although he had many financial setbacks when he was younger, Greeley was doing very well with the *New York Tribune*. If there was a social issue in America that needed solving, Greeley was probably promoting the solution.

So Margaret moved to New York City. Although Boston was a big city, New York City was much larger. In fact, New York City was three times larger. Now that Margaret was living in New York City, she looked forward to working for a prestigious newspaper.

The New York Tribune published many of the articles Margaret wrote. When Margaret moved to New York City, she lived with Horace Greeley and his wife Mary. Since Greeley had a large home in Manhattan, there was plenty of room for her.

One thing Margaret noticed about the Greeleys was that they only ate foods they thought were healthy. The Greeleys followed the Graham diet, which didn't allow them to eat many of the foods that most people enjoy. The Greeleys realized that Margaret was a grown woman, so they didn't expect her to live the way that they did.

Margaret made many new friends in New York City and she was glad that she had moved there. Sometimes she was sad, though, when she realized how many poor people lived in this big city.

Margaret was very impressed with Greeley, and she knew that he had faith in her abilities. So she began working on her first *Tribune* article, to review some of Ralph Waldo Emerson's essays. Needless to say, this would be a friendly review.

In addition to writing for the New York Tribune, Margaret was also working on her second book, titled *Woman in the Nineteenth Century*. Margaret was proud of this book and thought it was even better than her first book.

Many people were upset with her book, since she insisted that women should have the same rights as men. Some women thought Margaret was too outspoken. Most women, even if they believed in women's rights, wouldn't have had the courage to publish a book like this. Horace Greeley loved her book, so Margaret didn't have to worry about losing her job with the *New York Tribune*. Indeed, Greeley even helped Margaret publish it.

Woman in the Nineteenth Century presented ideas that Margaret had been thinking about for a few years. She had written an essay on this topic in *The Dial* magazine in 1843. However when Margaret expanded her essay into a book two years later, it caused quite a stir.

In her book, Margaret called for the abolition of slavery. In those days, many people in the North knew slavery was wrong. Unfortunately, many Americans in the Southern States wanted to continue owning slaves. Margaret definitely had no sympathy for slave-owners.

Nathaniel Hawthorne, who had been Margaret's friend, turned against her after the publication of this book. Margaret's feminism was too much for him. Hawthorne's wife, Sophia, was also opposed to this book. Margaret felt bad that some of her former friends were becoming her enemies.

However, many people liked her book. For instance, the literary critic Edgar Allan Poe was impressed by Margaret's book. Her friend Henry David Thoreau also wrote positive things about her book. Whether or not people liked her writing, Margaret had the need to express herself.

In addition to being a talented writer, she was a brilliant conversationalist. Many people believed Margaret was more talented in speaking than in writing. One thing Margaret particularly enjoyed was attending a salon hosted by Anne Charlotte Lynch.

Even though Anne was five years younger than Margaret, she had already created the top literary gathering place in America. On Saturday nights, everybody who was anybody went to Anne's home.

Anne Lynch lived with her mother, who was a widow. Anne's father died in a shipwreck when she was only fourteen years old. Anne's father was banished from Ireland for taking part in a rebellion. When her father was living in America, he met her mother and they had two children. These children were Thomas and Anne.

The people who attended Anne's salon felt welcome since she had an engaging personality. She liked to write, and was also a sculptor and a painter. Margaret and many other people looked forward to attending Anne's events. She felt like she was in her element when she attended these literary gatherings.

As enjoyable as Anne's weekly salon may have been, Margaret still needed to make a living. So she continued writing articles for the *New York Tribune*. She loved writing for this newspaper, because Horace Greeley let her write about a wide variety of topics.

The Elizabeth

In addition to writing articles and books, she also enjoyed writing poems. Margaret was always happy when she could share her ideas with others. She was satisfied with her writing career, yet she still hoped to be married someday.

Margaret didn't know if she would ever find a husband. She liked to flirt with men, but that was usually all it amounted to. Margaret sometimes wondered why marriage was so important to her. Besides looking for a man, there was something else Margaret wanted to do. She had always wanted to travel to Europe.

Before Margaret's father died she had planned on traveling to Europe. However, her father's death had put those plans on hold.

In the year 1846, she finally had the opportunity to travel to Europe. Horace Greeley was sending her there as a foreign correspondent for the *New York Tribune*.

Margaret Fuller was proud that she would be the first American woman who had ever done this type of work. So all that was left for her to do was prepare for her voyage to Europe. She was giddy with excitement, just imagining what it would be like to live in Europe. Her secret desire was to find romance in Europe.

CHAPTER 4
REVOLUTION

In 1846, Margaret set sail on the Cambria, a steamship that was able to make the voyage to Liverpool in only ten days. Margaret was now in England. She had finally achieved her goal of traveling to Europe.

Margaret Fuller knew that Ralph Waldo Emerson had met many important intellectuals when he traveled to Europe, and she was hoping to do the same. Although she was writing reports for the *New York Tribune*, Margaret financed her trip by working as a tutor.

A wealthy family had agreed to pay for Margaret's travel expenses if she would tutor their son Eddie. So Margaret traveled to Europe with Marcus, Rebecca, and Eddie Spring. In London, she discovered that her book, *Woman in the Nineteenth Century*, had also been published in England. Margaret was happy about this, because now more people would be aware of her writing.

The person Margaret was most interested in meeting was George Sand, the most popular writer in Europe. He was even more popular than Victor Hugo. Of course, George Sand was only her pen name. Sand's friends called her Aurore. She lived in France and Margaret wanted to interview her for the *New York Tribune*.

The Elizabeth

Margaret traveled to France, showed up at Aurore's home, knocked on the door, and was greeted by a servant girl. Since Margaret was still learning French, she was nervous about talking to people in that language. Someday she would improve her ability to speak French, but this wasn't that day.

To make matters worse, Madame Sand's servant didn't know much English. So her servant didn't pronounce Margaret's name correctly. Just when it seemed that Margaret wasn't going to get an interview, Madame Sand appeared and granted her an interview.

Margaret was fascinated with Sand's appearance – she was a large woman with an olive complexion. Although Sand was French, she had actually been born in Spain. By blood, Madame Sand was half French.

Almost immediately, Margaret and Aurore became friends. Although Margaret was interviewing Aurore for the *Tribune*, their conversation went beyond what was necessary for a standard interview.

At one point during the interview, Margaret asked Aurore about her radical views on sexuality. Aurore responded with, "In France, things are much different than in America. Something that might seem shocking in America is considered normal over here."

Margaret thought about this and decided there must be some truth to what Aurore said. She spent a long time talking to Aurore that day. Aurore was an impressive woman whom she was happy to count as one of her friends.

Another important person Margaret interviewed was Giuseppe Mazzini, who was living in exile in England. Margaret had interviewed Mazzini, before she traveled to France. He was an Italian revolutionary who often got arrested.

In those days, Italy was controlled by foreign countries. However, Mazzini wanted his country to be free from the influence of foreign powers. The country Italians hated the most was Austria, since it always stood in the way of a unified Italy.

Margaret Fuller admired Mazzini and believed that Italy should be unified. Mazzini even convinced Margaret to take secret papers to Italy. Without fully understanding why, Margaret was becoming a revolutionary.

So in 1847 Margaret traveled to Rome while was still working as a tutor. She loved tutoring Eddie Spring, who was only nine years old. Margaret enjoyed sharing her knowledge with others. The young boy's family was very good to Margaret and she needed their financial support in order to continue living in Europe.

Margaret had been in Rome for a week when she met Giovanni Ossoli, an Italian nobleman ten years younger than her. Giovanni was a supporter of Giuseppe Mazzini. Margaret didn't intend on falling in love with Giovanni, but she did.

The Elizabeth

Although Giovanni was part of Italian nobility, he didn't have much money. He was disinherited because he believed Italy should be unified. It was painful for Giovanni to be at odds with his family, but he had to do what he thought was right.

Ordinarily, Margaret wouldn't have been attracted to Giovanni since he wasn't an intellectual and he spoke very little English. However, she had become a revolutionary, and she also believed Italy should be unified.

Giovanni was a soldier and Margaret admired his bravery. She believed there was going to be a revolution in Italy and hoped the revolution would be successful. There were powerful forces, though, that wanted to keep things the way they were.

During these tumultuous times, Giovanni became Margaret's lover. At first, she thought this would only be a brief affair. However, when she became pregnant, she realized Giovanni meant more to her than she thought.

In order to keep her pregnancy a secret, Margaret moved away from Rome. She moved to an obscure Italian location so that only Giovanni and she would know about the pregnancy. Although Margaret was already 37 years old, she was looking forward to being a mother.

When Margaret had to leave Giovanni in the spring of 1848, not only was there revolution in Italy, but also in much of Europe. The European Revolution had started in

Sicily in January and quickly spread. Then, in February, revolution broke out in France and King Louis Phillippe was forced from the throne.

Margaret felt privileged to be living in Europe at this time. Most Americans living in Europe at this time were frightened by the revolutions taking place. Many of them were tourists, who only wanted to have a nice vacation.

However, Margaret seemed to thrive on danger. She hoped with all her heart that her readers back in America would understand the importance of the Italian Revolution. Margaret wished she could do more to help unify Italy, but she was only one person.

At the same time revolutions were happening in Europe, changes were also taking place in America. In July of 1848, a Women's Rights convention was held in Seneca Falls, New York. Both women and men attended this two-day event. This was one event Margaret regretted not being able to witness in person.

Three hundred people attended this convention, and 100 people signed the Declaration of Sentiments. Even Frederick Douglass spoke at this convention. However, Margaret believed she was where she should be. She was already well into her pregnancy and she was looking forward to holding her baby in her arms.

In Italy, the soldiers from the Austrian Empire were trying to keep control of Italy. This was because Austria made money from Italy by harshly taxing the Italians. Margaret was sad when she saw the way the Italian people were being treated.

Then, in late July, the Italians lost a major battle in northern Italy, the Battle of Custoza. The Italian soldiers were having a difficult time fighting against the Austrian Empire because Austria had a powerful army.

In Rome, though, the Revolutionaries were more successful. Pope Pius IX initially supported the Revolution. Pius IX had only been the Pope for two years and Margaret hoped he would continue to support the Italian Revolution.

Margaret was forced to take a momentary break from politics when her son was born in September of 1838. Margaret was happy when she held Angelo. Although Margaret enjoyed being a mother, she wanted to be with Giovanni again. She also planned to continue writing articles for the *New York Tribune* as a war correspondent and it was dangerous work, so she found a wet nurse for Angelo and returned to Rome.

Things seemed to be going reasonably well in Rome until the Pope's secretary was assassinated. The Revolutionaries hated Pius's secretary because he was trying to prevent any real change from happening. Then the Pope was put under house arrest since many of the Revolutionaries didn't trust him, either. There was so much happening in the Italian Revolution, but Margaret Fuller never seemed to worry about her own safety.

CHAPTER 5
THE POPE

Pope Pius IX was under house arrest in Rome and he wasn't happy about it. He kept replaying the sequence of events that led to his current predicament. How could he, God's servant, be treated so shabbily? Pius had supported liberal reforms in Italy, but these Revolutionaries wanted too much.

They thought Italy could be like America, but this was never going to happen. You couldn't let everybody vote or you would have anarchy. Then Pius remembered that terrible day on November 15th when someone stabbed Pellegrino Rossi in the neck.

Rossi was the Pope's personal secretary and he had only been trying to help Pius. The Pope thought to himself, "These revolutionaries actually seem to be happy that my personal secretary was killed. Don't these people have any respect?"

In those days, the Pope lived in the Quirinal Palace. However, now that the Swiss Guard had been disarmed, Pius no longer felt secure. How could he, now that he no longer had armed bodyguards protecting him? Pius knew he could no longer live like this and he wondered how he could escape from Rome.

The Elizabeth

The Pope prayed that God would show him how to escape from his house arrest. Since Pius was God's humble servant, he knew God would help him. After a short time, Pius began to plan how he could outwit these radicals. Nine days after the assassination of his secretary, the Pope escaped from Rome.

First, Pius disguised himself as an ordinary priest. Then, with the help of foreign Ambassadors, he was able to sneak out of the palace.

Soon, the revolutionaries discovered that the Pope was missing. Where could he have gone? It turned out that Pius was now living in Gaeta, under the protection of Ferdinand II. Gaeta was 75 miles from Rome and located on the Mediterranean Sea.

Now that the Pope was no longer a prisoner, he was able to think more clearly. The radicals might temporarily have the upper hand, but Pius knew that he would soon regain control of Rome. Pius still couldn't believe how arrogant the revolutionaries were. They didn't love God or his representative.

When Pius had been in Rome, the revolutionaries constantly pressured him to make decisions he didn't agree with. Now Pius felt free to tell the world about the way he had been mistreated. The revolutionaries tried to negotiate with him, but Pius wasn't going to cooperate with them.

Any decisions the revolutionaries made without his consent, he refused to recognize. It made the Pope happy when he remembered he had the power to excommunicate any Catholic who didn't agree with him. One of the people Pius wanted to excommunicate was Margaret Fuller.

The Pope became angry when he read her articles in the *New York Tribune*. Pius was shocked that an American woman would criticize him in a major newspaper. Unfortunately, though, he wouldn't be able to kick Margaret out of the Catholic church since she wasn't Catholic.

Then the Pope tried to think of something that would cheer him up. It was difficult staying positive when there were so many people who wanted to defy him. "I should be living in Rome, not Gaeta," Pius angrily thought. He was further surprised when the radicals declared a Roman Republic.

The three leaders of the Republic were Giuseppe Mazzini, Carlo Armellini, and Aurelio Saffi. These radicals actually believed that they could replace Pius' Papal States with their own government. These revolutionaries were never satisfied with small reforms. This is exactly why he had never trusted the radicals in Rome.

The Italian radical the pope hated the most was Giuseppe Mazzini, who had a history of being a troublemaker. Mazzini had been trying to unify Italy for many years. Usually, Mazzini was either living in exile or he was in jail. However, now Giuseppe Mazzini was the most important leader of the Roman Republic.

The Elizabeth

The Pope didn't like Giuseppe Garibaldi, either. Garibaldi was a military man who was always starting a rebellion. Not satisfied with causing problems in Europe, he had also fought in rebellions in South America.

Garibaldi had a wife who was Brazilian and she had fought with her husband in some of the rebellions. Now Garibaldi was in charge of the military for the Roman Republic. Pius knew he wouldn't be able to return to Rome until Garibaldi was defeated.

However, not everybody was helping Mazzini and Garibaldi. Indeed, that very morning, Pius had met with Leopold II, a very powerful Italian ruler who was no longer helping the revolutionaries. The radicals had tried to get Leopold to help them fight against the Austrians.

Of course, he had refused, and now he was living with Pius in Gaeta. Although Pius hated to do it, he was going to have to ask the Austrians for a favor. So the Pope asked Austria to attack the Roman Republic and to restore his power in the Papal States.

The Austrians agreed to help the Pope because they didn't like the revolutionaries either. Pius knew that even with the Austrians helping him, it was going to be difficult regaining control of Rome. It wasn't easy being the Pope when the radicals constantly challenged his authority.

The Pope then told Leopold II, "That horrible man, Giuseppe Mazzini, has even confiscated some of the land that was owned by the church and gave it to the poor." Leopold replied, "I believe anything you tell me about these radicals. These are men who must be punished for their crimes."

The Roman Republic had abolished the death penalty. These revolutionaries were reforming the Papal States in ways that Pius couldn't accept. The Pope thought to himself, "These radicals must be defeated."

The Austrian military was achieving great victories in northern Italy, but they weren't ready to attack Rome. Pius knew the Austrians were doing their best to help him. However, Austria had their own problems. There was a revolution going on in Hungary, so the Austrians were also fighting against the Hungarians.

The Pope thought to himself, "The whole world seems to be at war."

Then suddenly, Pius received news that France was going to help him. Pius felt good, because he knew God was on his side. God was rewarding him for his obedience. The Pope also knew that the revolutionaries wouldn't stand a chance against Louis Napoleon.

Louis Napoleon was Napoleon's nephew. Since Napoleon I was no longer living, Louis Napoleon was now the President of France. When French troops arrived in Italy, Pius felt confident that he would soon be returning to Rome. The French forces were led by Charles Oudinot. It was April of 1849 when Oudinot attacked Garibaldi. Although

Oudinot had a larger Army, they lost the battle againt Garibaldi.

Fortunately for Oudinot, additional soldiers arrived from France a few days later, so Oudinot continued fighting against Garibaldi.

Although Garibaldi was a more talented General than Oudinot, that didn't matter since Oudinot had unlimited resources. Gradually the French forces began to advance on Rome.

Indeed, by June, the entire city of Rome was under siege. The French positioned their artillery in key locations and it was only a matter of time before they would conquer Rome. The Austrians continued taking over other parts of Italy. The Pope felt good that finally things were improving.

Giuseppe Garibaldi knew he was defeated, but he refused to give up. Garibaldi was going to fight to the bitter end. Pope Pius couldn't figure out why Garibaldi was so stubborn. However, by July 1, 1849, the French had conquered Rome. Even though the French were now in control of Rome, Garibaldi never surrendered to them.

Instead, the Italian General left Rome and took some of his troops with him. Though Pius hoped Garibaldi would be captured, this hadn't happened yet. Giuseppe Mazzini had also escaped from Rome. Although Pius knew that these two men were no longer an immediate threat to him, he was still upset that they had escaped from Rome.

CHAPTER 6
COURAGE

Margaret Fuller had plenty to do after the Roman Republic was declared in February of 1849. Although she hoped that the Republic would succeed, her intellect told her it probably wouldn't. Giovanni was serving as a soldier for the Roman Republic and Margaret was proud that her lover was a brave man.

Margaret was also a courageous woman who volunteered to work at a hospital and care for wounded soldiers. She quickly realized that she had more courage than she thought. Indeed, before long, she was asked to be the director of a hospital. Margaret was honored to serve in this position.

Margaret loved Giovanni and she knew that he wanted to marry her. So it wasn't long before they filled out the paperwork and were officially married. Sometimes Margaret felt awkward when she realized that her husband was ten years younger than she.

Although Giovanni fought bravely with his regiment, the French military was too powerful for the Roman Republic. So when the soldiers of the Republic had been defeated, Margaret and Giovanni left Rome. Thankfully, Margaret had secretly obtained an American passport for Giovanni.

The Elizabeth

If it wasn't for this passport, it is unlikely that Giovanni would have been able to leave Rome. Indeed, even with the passport, he was briefly detained. Now Margaret and Giovanni needed to travel to Rieti, fifty miles from Rome, to be reunited with their baby Angelo.

On the way to Rieti, Margaret said to Giovanni, "I can't wait to see our son again." Giovanni replied, "I haven't even seen little Angelo yet. Although I'm sad that the Roman Republic no longer exists, at least now we can be a family."

Margaret responded, "As long as the Republic is alive in our hearts, it will always exist. Indeed, the next book I write will be about the Roman Republic. I promise you that this will be the best book I have ever written."

Giovanni was proud that Margaret had shown bravery during her stay in Rome. She had cared for wounded soldiers and written for an American newspaper as a war correspondent. Although most men were frightened of a strong woman, Giovanni was not.

When Margaret and Giovanni arrived in Rieti, their first priority was to see little Angelo. They were shocked when they saw that their baby was sick. The wet nurse hadn't cared for Angelo properly and now his parents would need to nurse him back to health.

The wet nurse slipped away when she saw that Margaret and Giovanni were worried about their son. That day Giovanni prayed that if God would help his son regain his health, he would do everything in his power to protect Angelo and Margaret. This was one of the few days of Giovanni's life when he openly wept.

Before long, baby Angelo began to recover and the Ossoli family traveled north of Rieti to Florence, a long journey of 163 miles.

Under ordinary circumstances, Margaret would have loved living in Florence. However, since she had become a Revolutionary, she was more worried about the safety of her family. Although the Ossoli family was no longer threatened by the French military, now they faced danger from the Austrians. The Austrian secret police was a powerful force in Florence and they didn't like revolutionaries.

Margaret told Giovanni, "I don't know how long we will be able to live in Florence." Giovanni replied, "I would like to leave, but we have run out of money. We will have to keep a low profile until we have enough money to move somewhere else."

She knew why they didn't have any money. It was because Giovanni had been disinherited by his family for being a revolutionary, and she wasn't making much money either.

Margaret didn't blame Giovanni or herself for their current predicament. How could she? They were simply two people who had to live their lives according to their convictions. However, she did worry for the safety of Angelo.

The Elizabeth

So Margaret decided to begin seriously working on her new book. This would be the best book she had ever written. She would write about the Italian Revolution. Although the revolution had failed, this was a story that needed to be told. "Someday," she thought, "Italy will be unified."

Until then, Margaret would have to be satisfied with writing her book. She knew Giovanni would appreciate a book about a cause for which he had sacrificed everything. Margaret wanted the world to know the true story of the Italian Revolution and the fall of the Roman Republic.

In many ways, Margaret Ossoli knew she was the person who was most qualified to write this book. Not only was she an intellectual, she had also been an eyewitness to this part of history. Most talented writers would never have placed themselves in the middle of a Revolution. However, Margaret Ossoli showed exceptional bravery while she was in Italy.

Even after Margaret and her family escaped from Rome, there there were further developments in the story she was writing. The most dramatic event was that Giuseppe Garibaldi refused to surrender to the French. Garibaldi took some of his soldiers and marched out of Rome.

Any hopes that Garibaldi had for continuing to fight for Italian unification were quickly destroyed. The French, Austrians, and others were chasing him. Most of Garibaldi's troops abandoned him and his pregnant wife died while trying to escape from Italy with her husband.

A lesser man would have been captured, but somehow Garibaldi escaped to North Africa. As excited as Margaret was that he had escaped from Italy, she knew she had to write the other parts of her book first. That was all right, though, because Margaret didn't mind spending her time writing such an important book.

When Margaret was living in Florence, she had the opportunity to meet the Brownings. Elizabeth Barrett Browning and Robert Browning were famous British poets who lived in Florence. Elizabeth's father disinherited her for marrying Robert.

She still had enough money to live comfortably in Italy, but Elizabeth had sacrificed a lot for love. At the age of 43, Elizabeth Barrett Browning became a mother for the first time. Her son had a fancy name, but everyone just called him Pen. Elizabeth and Robert were devoted parents who wanted the best for their child.

Baby Pen was three months younger than baby Angelo. Margaret was always happy when she saw the two babies playing together so nicely. As time went by, Margaret found herself spending more time visiting with the Brownings.

Although the Brownings were quite liberal, they weren't radical, like Margaret had become. Despite their political differences, Margaret got along quite well with Elizabeth and Robert. She felt bad, though, because Elizabeth was sick all the time.

The Elizabeth

Elizabeth was constantly ill for a variety of reasons. One of the reasons was due to a recent miscarriage. However, sometimes Elizabeth pretended to be sicker than she was so she wouldn't have to meet new people. Margaret thought Elizabeth was a complicated, yet very talented poet.

Margaret knew she would miss the Brownings when she and her family left Florence. Indeed, Margaret and Giovanni were planning to move to America. Margaret found it hard to believe that little Angelo was going to be raised in America.

CHAPTER 7
MARBLE

There is a very interesting city in Italy called Carrara, located 76 miles from Florence. It is famous for its marble. Indeed, the finest marble in the world is quarried there. Even Michelangelo sculpted with Carrara marble. This marble was so highly prized that people outside of Italy also wanted to buy it.

Fortunately, the Marble Mountains where the marble was quarried, isn't very far from the Mediterranean. This made it possible to ship Carrara marble to other parts of the world. An American freighter called The Elizabeth was planning to ship a large amount of this marble to America.

By coincidence, Margaret and Giovanni had decided that their family would sail to America on The Elizabeth. Although it wasn't a passenger ship, this was the least expensive way for the Ossoli family to travel to America.

Even though Margaret's close friend, Ralph Waldo Emerson had offered to pay her way on a passenger ship, she preferred to do things on her own. So the Ossoli family traveled to Livorno, which was a journey of 55 miles. Margaret had also hired a young Italian girl named Celeste to help care for Angelo on the voyage to America.

The Elizabeth

Family friend Robert Browning traveled with the Ossoli's to Livorno. Margaret and Giovanni made small talk with Robert while they waited for their ship. It was nice, Margaret thought, that Robert went out of his way to say goodbye to them.

When The Elizabeth arrived and Robert saw how low it was sailing in the water, he became alarmed. He said, "Margaret, I beg of you, please don't sail on that ship." Margaret replied, "Why do you say that?" To which Robert responded, "Look at how low The Elizabeth is sailing in the water. This ship is overloaded with marble. It isn't safe for you or your family to sail on this ship."

Margaret wished Robert hadn't said this. Since she didn't know how to swim, Margaret was already nervous about the voyage to America. However, Robert continued his efforts of trying to convince her not to sail on the ship, saying, "There has to be another way for you to travel to America."

Margaret's mind was made up, though, so she said her goodbyes to Robert Browning. Then the Ossoli family boarded The Elizabeth. Since Margaret was used to traveling on passenger ships, it seemed odd that there weren't very many people on The Elizabeth. This ship was clearly designed for hauling cargo rather than passengers.

Margaret felt more confident, though, after she met the ship's captain. Seth Hasty seemed to be a man who knew his trade. As The Elizabeth began to leave Livorno, Margaret,

Giovanni, and baby Angelo waved to Robert Browning. When Margaret saw Robert waving back, she began to wonder if her family really should be sailing on this ship.

It was May 7, 1850, when the Ossoli family set sail for America. As Margaret held her son she thought, "It's hard to believe that Angelo is already twenty months old." She and Giovanni wanted to live in New York City since that was where many Italian-Americans lived. Margaret could now speak Italian fluently, so she was excited to return to New York City with Giovanni and baby Angelo.

The voyage to America began smoothly enough. There was a passenger on The Elizabeth, named Horace Sumner. He was a young man from a politically well-connected family. His father had been involved in politics, but was no longer living. However, Sumner's older brother Charles was beginning to make a name for himself in the political world.

Margaret was already familiar with Horace Sumner since they had become good friends during her time in Florence. Horace had traveled to Italy because he hoped that the climate would be good for his health. Margaret could sympathize with him, since she had struggled with her own health issues.

Margaret also liked the Captain's wife. Catherine Hasty was a young and vibrant woman. Margaret felt good knowing there were some interesting people to visit with on The Elizabeth. If there was one thing Margaret enjoyed, it was conversation.

The Elizabeth

The crew members on the ship were also very kind. Indeed, the Captain and the crew were always very playful with baby Angelo. Everything was going so well that Margaret wondered why she had been so worried about making this journey.

Then tragedy struck. Captain Hasty became infected with smallpox and died in Gibraltar. When baby Angelo also became infected with smallpox, Margaret and Giovanni were terrified. Margaret had some experience in caring for wounded soldiers in Italy, but she certainly wasn't a doctor.

Suddenly, Giovanni regained his courage. He said to Margaret, "We must pray for our son." Ordinarily, Margaret wouldn't have agreed to this, but she was so worried about Angelo that she was willing to try anything.

Giovanni continued, "When Angelo was sick before, I prayed for him and God healed him." Margaret replied, "This time we will both pray for our son." So that is what they did. They also both nursed Angelo to the best of their ability. Mrs. Hasty, although she was grieving over the loss of her husband, was terribly worried about Angelo. Indeed, everybody on The Elizabeth was pulling for the little toddler.

On this 530 ton vessel, there were six passengers and fourteen crew members. The Elizabeth was also hauling one-hundred tons of marble, as well as a statue of John C. Calhoun. Earlier in the voyage, Margaret had considered tossing the marble bust into the sea. She hated Senator

Calhoun even more than she hated the Pope. She thought, "Why should such a horrible man be honored with a statue?" The fact that Calhoun had been dead for a few months didn't make her feel any better about the statue.

Margaret had confided to Horace Sumner, "I wish someone would toss this marble statue into the Mediterranean." Horace responded, "No one despises that slave-owning bastard more than I do, but that isn't the right thing to do." After Horace said this, Margaret decided to give up her plot of harming the marble bust.

Margaret admired Horace since he was opposed to the Mexican-American war that had taken place in 1848. Horace was always telling Margaret that she must meet his brother Charles. He idolized Charles, and he knew that Margaret would also be impressed with him.

After some time had passed, little Angelo made a full recovery from his smallpox. Needless to say, Margaret and Giovanni were greatly relieved. Now they would be able to arrive in America with their entire family.

Angelo was her pride and joy, and Margaret looked forward to showing him to her mother. Margaret thought, "God, please grant me one more wish. Let me look at my mother's face one more time."

CHAPTER 8
FAMILY AND FRIENDS

Back in America, Margaret's family was excited that she was returning to see them. Her mother, who was also named Margaret, couldn't stop talking about her new grandson. Although Mrs. Fuller loved her daughter, it was Angelo she really wanted to see.

Mrs. Fuller was also pleased that Margaret was beginning to achieve happiness with a family of her own, though. Margaret's siblings were looking forward to her return, too. She had been in Europe for four years, and they missed their big sister. They all remembered when Margaret had been their babysitter and supervised their education. Margaret's father had taught her so well, that he decided she would be in charge of teaching her siblings.

Margaret, of course, wanted to educate others. Sometimes, though, she suffered from terrible migraines. This made it difficult for her to do everything she wanted to do. In those days, she taught Eugene, William, Ellen, Richard, and James. Since women weren't allowed to attend college, Margaret had prepared her brothers for Harvard. Her sister, Ellen, of course, couldn't attend college.

When Margaret had lived in America, she had always done her best, to help educate other women. Indeed, Margaret

The Elizabeth

had been a true champion of Women's Rights. So there were many women in America who were also looking forward to Margaret's return.

Conversely, there were some women in America who hated Margaret Ossoli. This is because Margaret was outspoken and often said or wrote things they disagreed with. Although Margaret enjoyed having friends, she knew she couldn't make everyone happy.

Ralph Waldo Emerson also wanted to see Margaret again. He greatly admired her intellect and missed their conversations. Emerson sent Margaret many letters when she was in Europe, but he had actually discouraged Margaret from returning to America.

This was because Emerson knew there would be new challenges Margaret would have to face in America. Margaret had been a controversial person before she went to Europe. And while in Europe, not only did she participate in the Italian Revolution, she even denounced the Pope.

However, Ralph Waldo Emerson had also ruffled a few feathers in his time. He certainly wasn't going to turn his back on Margaret simply because there were some people who didn't like her. Emerson also wanted to see the manuscript of the book Margaret had written.

As The Elizabeth continued on its voyage to America, many people were excited that Margaret was returning. In Europe, though, many were saddened by her departure.

Margaret herself had mixed emotions about leaving Europe. She had been in Europe for four years, and yet there was still so much she wanted to see and do.

Giovanni Ossoli also had many thoughts running through his mind. He was happy to be traveling to America with his wife and son. Now that the Italian Revolution had been crushed, it made more sense to live in America. However, Margaret had told Giovanni that not everything was perfect in America.

Giovanni also knew that he was going to miss his family back in Italy. Though his radical beliefs had strained his relationship with his family, he still loved them. Giovanni hoped that one day he could be reconciled with his mother, brothers and sisters.

It broke his heart that political differences had separated him from his family. He hadn't wanted that. Giovanni had a different vision for the future of Italy than the rest of his family. Indeed, Giovanni still wanted to liberate his country from the domination of the Austrians and the French.

Though Giovanni was Catholic, he could never forgive the Pope for destroying the Roman Republic. Giovanni still attended church services even though he didn't approve of Pope Pius IX. Margaret didn't care for the Catholic church, but she showed respect for Giovanni by going to church with him. This was something that he greatly appreciated.

Sometimes Margaret wondered why Giovanni loved her. She was ten years older than him, and for most men, that would have been a deal-breaker. For some reason, though, Giovanni adored Margaret. She felt fortunate to have finally found someone who loved her as she was.

As The Elizabeth continued to sail toward America, the passengers and crew members began to think about what they would do when they reached New York City. It was always exciting to visit New York City, since that was the biggest city in America. However, not everything in New York City was praiseworthy.

Like most big cities, there were many poor people living there. When Margaret had lived in New York City, she had pointed out that the women's prisons needed to be reformed. She had visited the women's prisons and spoken directly with the prisoners. She had done her best to speak words of encouragement to these ladies.

The women were happy to meet Margaret and listened carefully to what she said. *The New York Tribune* published articles Margaret wrote about the need for prison reform. Margaret had a kind heart and hated to see people mistreated. When she visited the women prisoners, she advised them to prepare themselves for the outside world.

Margaret did this because her heart was filled with compassion for these ladies. She wanted these women to make good decisions, so after they were released from these wretched prisons they wouldn't have to return. Margaret thought, "No woman should ever have to stay in this type of a prison."

Foremost in Margaret's mind, though, was her intention to publish her manuscript about the Roman Revolution. During the previous year, she had written a letter to her brother Richard explaining the importance of this book.

Of course, at that time, Margaret's manuscript had been a work in progress. Now her manuscript was finished and Margaret was certain that someone in America would be willing to publish it. As The Elizabeth got closer to New York City, Margaret began to wonder how her new book would be received by the public.

When Horace Greeley published Margaret's book, *Woman In The Nineteenth Century*, it sold quite well even though it was a controversial book. However, Margaret knew that her new book about the Roman Republic would also upset some people. Whether people liked her new book or hated it, Margaret intended to publish it.

While holding Angelo, Margaret thought to herself, "He is such a beautiful and happy child who always wants to please his mother. I am fortunate to have such an amazing son." When Margaret looked at Angelo, though, she began to think of another child she had been fond of.

This child's name was Waldo, and he was Ralph Waldo Emerson's son. Waldo always had something profound to say. Margaret had been astonished by Waldo's wisdom. Of course, most adults would never have listened attentively to him the way that Margaret did.

The Elizabeth

Sadly, though, Waldo died while he was still young. Of course, everyone who knew the small boy was devastated. Even now, Margaret had tears in her eyes, as she thought about young Waldo. At that moment, Giovanni returned to their ship's cabin. He saw Margaret crying, and said, "What's wrong?"

Margaret responded, "I was just thinking about a dear friend who died." Giovanni replied, "Who is this dear friend?" Margaret said, "He was a young boy named Waldo who lived in America. I loved him more than I can express, but God took him from me at a very young age. Even though this happened a number of years ago, I don't think I will ever recover from it."

When Giovanni heard this, he embraced Margaret and said, "This is why I love you. There is no one who has a heart as tender as yours. If there were more people like you, this would be a much happier world. Our son is lucky to have such a loving mother."

SECTION II
THE ELIZABETH

CHAPTER 9
SHIPWRECKED

The Elizabeth continued her voyage to America. In just a few more days, the ship would arrive in New York City. After Captain Hasty died from smallpox, the responsibility of sailing The Elizabeth had fallen on first mate Bangs. It was a big responsibility, but so far everything was going smoothly.

Although he didn't have the experience Captain Hasty had, first mate Bangs felt confident he could safely sail The Elizabeth to New York City. Bangs and the crew not only needed to get their six passengers to America safely, but they were also transporting valuable cargo, important items like marble and silk needed to make it to America.

However, first mate Bangs also knew that the weather could change quickly on the Atlantic Ocean. He thought to himself, "I hope the weather stays good for just a few more days." The crew of The Elizabeth was thinking similar thoughts.

Horace Sumner, a friend of Margaret's, was ready to return to America. He had traveled to Italy hoping that the warm climate would improve his health. He was feeling much better now and was looking forward to seeing his brother Charles again.

The Elizabeth

Charles Sumner was a brilliant orator and a member of the Free Soil political party. Horace knew his brother would always fight for what was right, even if it was unpopular. In some ways, Margaret Ossoli reminded Horace of Charles, since both of them were uncompromising in their political beliefs.

They believed something was either right or it wasn't. Neither Margaret nor Charles worried about their personal safety. For instance, Margaret had written controversial books and been surrounded by warfare in Italy. Likewise, Charles Sumner had angered many people by opposing slavery.

It would never occur to Margaret or Charles to be careful about what they said. They didn't intentionally try to offend people, but they also weren't going to pretend that problems didn't exist in America. Margaret and Charles were willing to fight for the causes they believed in.

Although Horace Sumner had enjoyed his visit to Italy, he knew it was time to return to America. Horace realized he would never be the mover and shaker his brother was, but he still believed he had a role to play. Since Horace was only 25 years old, he still had many things he wanted to accomplish.

Another passenger who was deep in thought was Mrs. Hasty. Everything had seemed so promising when she first set sail on The Elizabeth. However, now her husband was dead and Mrs. Hasty was a widow. Everyone on the ship was kind to her, but that didn't prevent her from crying herself to sleep at night.

Then there was also Celeste Paolini. Celeste was Angelo's nursemaid. She was the young Italian girl Margaret and Giovanni had hired to care for their son. Margaret was very pleased with how Celeste was helping out with Angelo. Celeste was hoping to make a new life for herself in America and she thought, "America is the land of opportunity and I will be happy there."

On the evening of July 18, 1850, first mate Bangs told the passengers to pack their belongings. This was because they would be arriving in New York City the next morning. It had been a long voyage and everyone was happy to hear they had almost reached their destination.

That evening, as Margaret was holding Angelo and talking to Giovanni she said, "I'm glad you are going to meet my family in America. I must warn you, though, all my mother cares about is seeing her new grandson." Angelo laughed when he heard this.

Although he was only a toddler, he was old enough to understand that he was going to be meeting his grandmother. Angelo was also happy because he knew that his parents were excited. "Grandma, Grandma," Angelo said. Margaret and Giovanni laughed when they heard their son say this.

Angelo was so innocent. That was why all the sailors on The Elizabeth had enjoyed becoming friends with him.

The Elizabeth

Both Margaret and Giovanni believed that Angelo would one day achieve great things. They also noticed how their little toddler left a good impression on everyone who met him.

As the passengers of the ship got ready for bed, there was an unusually strong wind. Few of the passengers, though, were alarmed. They figured they had made it this far in their voyage, so they could make it the rest of the way. First mate Bangs, though, was concerned with the sudden change of weather.

He knew that now it would be more difficult to safely sail The Elizabeth to New York City. Since Bangs didn't want anyone to panic, he kept his thoughts to himself. He thought, "There is no point in alarming the crew and passengers unless we are in an emergency situation."

Margaret was also concerned about the sudden strength of the wind. Since she didn't know how to swim, she was always a bit fearful of the water and now she had other people to think about. "If anything happens to Angelo or Giovanni," Margaret thought, "I will never forgive myself."

Although, Angelo and Giovanni were sleeping soundly, she knew she would have a sleepless night. Margaret was now very upset and wishing that she had never sailed on The Elizabeth. As the evening progressed, the weather worsened and Margaret's fear increased until she was terrified.

Now first mate Bangs wasn't just concerned, he was genuinely worried. The strong winds had turned into a terrible storm and this was the type of storm that caused shipwrecks. Bangs thought to himself, "If only Captain Hasty was here, he would know what to do."

However, first mate Bangs knew that it was up to him to safely sail the ship. The gale force winds, though, were not making this an easy task. Although Bangs thought he knew where he was, he actually didn't. For instance, when he saw a lighthouse, he thought it was a different lighthouse.

After Bangs became confused about where he was, he sailed The Elizabeth in the wrong direction. It was 3:30 AM on July 19, 1850, and the wind was howling. Now, for the first time, Bangs and the crew realized the true danger they were facing.

Just as the first mate and crew were thinking these dreary thoughts, The Elizabeth ran aground on a sandbar. The impact of The Elizabeth hitting the sandbar caused quite a jolt. If anyone on the ship had been sleeping, they weren't now. Although everything was turning out badly, first mate Bangs was still trying to make the best of a bad situation.

Inside The Elizabeth, Carrara marble crashed and broke the knees of the ship. Although The Elizabeth had shipwrecked only three hundred yards from Fire Island in New York, it might as well have been thirty miles away. The storm was unrelenting and even an experienced swimmer would have difficulty swimming to shore under these conditions.

The Elizabeth

First mate Bangs thought to himself, "If only the storm would let up," even as he knew that this was unlikely to happen anytime soon. The Elizabeth was severely damaged, and could only offer the passengers and crew minimal protection from the storm.

At this point the marble and silk that The Elizabeth was hauling, no longer mattered to first mate Bangs. His first priority was to help the passengers and crew make it safely to shore. Gale force winds buffeted the ship and large waves crashed against what remained of The Elizabeth.

Luckily, nobody had drowned yet, but Bangs realized that drowning was a real possibility. If the passengers and crew could make it safely to shore, he would be satisfied. Bangs certainly hoped nobody on The Elizabeth would die.

The passengers on the ship were frightened and Angelo cried when he felt the strong wind and cold rain from the storm. He could also see the fear in his mother's eyes. Something wasn't right, but Angelo's mother was too frightened to comfort him. His nursemaid Celeste was also crying, so that made Angelo cry even more.

When first mate Bangs looked once again to the shore, he hoped that the people on Fire Island would help the passengers and crew of The Elizabeth. He was outraged, though, when he noticed that nobody was making any attempt to rescue them. Instead, those people were only interested in plundering the valuable cargo they saw washing ashore.

CHAPTER 10
THE WRECKERS

The people taking the cargo washing ashore were opportunists. They had no legal right to the cargo, but they were taking it anyway. These people weren't innocent beachcombers, they were wreckers.

However, first mate Bangs knew that his first priority was to get the people on The Elizabeth to safety. So he couldn't allow himself to be distracted by worrying about the wreckers. Even though the wreckers were obnoxious, they could be dealt with later.

Since nobody from shore was helping them, Bangs decided to let one of his crew members make an attempt to swim to shore. This crew member donned a life-jacket and successfully made it to Fire Island. Then another crew member grabbed a piece of wood, and jumped into the turbulent water.

It was quite a battle, but somehow he also made it to shore. First mate Bangs thought to himself, "This approach might work for strong swimmers, but what about everybody else?" Just then, two of the passengers volunteered to make an attempt to swim to shore. The volunteers were Catherine Hasty and Horace Sumner.

The Elizabeth

Mrs. Hasty, the young widow made it to shore, but Horace Sumner drowned. After witnessing the drowning, the other passengers decided to wait for help. However, remaining on a ship that was severely damaged was also dangerous. Surely, there was a lifeboat somewhere on Fire Island that would rescue them.

Finally, a lifeboat appeared on shore. The storm was so strong, though, that nobody was willing to attempt the rescue. As The Elizabeth continued to disintegrate, first mate Bangs decided it was too dangerous for anyone to remain on the ship.

Bangs had thought of a plan to help the four remaining passengers make it to shore with the assistance of crew members. However, since Margaret, Giovanni, and Celeste didn't know how to swim, they were too frightened to leave the ship.

One of the crew members took Angelo and tried to swim to shore with the toddler. Tragically, both of them drowned and Angelo's body was washed to the shore of Fire Island. Everyone who had safely made it to shore was devastated when they saw the toddler's lifeless body.

Angelo had been everybody's favorite. It was one thing to have the silk was ashore and be plundered by the wreckers. It was quite another, though, to see a tiny boy who had lost his life. It didn't seem fair that someone who was so innocent would have to perish.

Back on The Elizabeth, the ship continued to fall apart. The gamble Margaret, Giovanni, and Celeste took in remaining onboard turned into a losing proposition. The Elizabeth could no longer protect them and they were thrown into the raging sea.

Since there was nobody to help them and they didn't know how to swim, all three of them drowned. Not only did they drown, but Margaret Ossoli's manuscript also vanished. Sadly, eight people on The Elizabeth were killed by the storm.

Margaret, Giovanni and Celeste's bodies were never found. The toddler Angelo had adored Celeste, but the storm had cruelly taken her life. The survivors of The Elizabeth were grief-stricken when they thought about their dear friends who had drowned.

What made matters worse for the survivors, was seeing the greedy wreckers taking things that did not belong to them. The wreckers only cared about money. They had no compassion for the suffering of others. However, Captain Bangs thought to himself, "If there is a God in heaven, these wreckers will pay for what they have done."

Word of the tragedy traveled fast even though it had just taken place. It wasn't long before Horace Greeley, Margaret's employer at the *New York Tribune* learned that Margaret lost her life. She had also lived in his mansion for a time so he knew here well. At first, he couldn't believe she was gone. Margaret Ossoli was a larger than life force. But

The Elizabeth

even she was mortal. Greeley thought about the irony of her surviving the war in Italy only to be killed by a storm.

Another person who quickly learned about Margaret's death was Ralph Waldo Emerson. He was in anguish when he realized he would never be able to speak to Margaret again. It had been a long time since his heart was this heavy. Emerson immediately contacted Henry David Thoreau.

Thoreau had never seen Emerson this frantic before. Emerson told him, "Margaret Ossoli died in a shipwreck off of Fire Island. I need you to travel there and find out the details of what actually happened." Although Thoreau didn't want to travel to New York, he agreed to do so when he saw how upset his friend was.

So he told Emerson, "I will leave at once." Emerson replied, "There is just one more thing. See if you can find the manuscript of the book Margaret wrote. It is the only copy of her book." When Thoreau arrived at Fire Island, he was very business-like in his approach. This was difficult, because Margaret was his friend.

He might not have been as close to her as Emerson, but that didn't mean he wasn't startled that she had drowned. Since Thoreau had always struggled with poor health, it made him consider his own mortality. However, Thoreau continually reminded himself that his purpose on Fire Island was to make a report of what had happened to The Elizabeth.

He would have to wait until he had completed the rough draft of his report before he could allow himself to grieve the loss of his dear friend. It wasn't fair that he was being forced to repress his emotions. However, it also wasn't fair that Margaret Ossoli had lost her life at the age of 40.

So Thoreau began interviewing the wreckers. Although he despised them, he had to keep his emotions in check. Since the wreckers were witnesses to the aftermath of the shipwreck, Thoreau would need to speak to them in order to give Emerson an accurate report.

After Thoreau sharpened his pencil, he began to take notes. Since, he didn't verbally attack the wreckers, Thoreau was able to get a frank account of the tragedy that had taken place. Although Thoreau wished that the lifeboat had been used to save Margaret Ossoli and the others, he also realized he might have felt differently if he had witnessed the storm.

It was easy to sit back in safety and say what should have happened. However, since Thoreau was braver than most, he knew in his heart that he would have made an attempt to rescue the passengers and crew on The Elizabeth. Thoreau also knew, though, that rescuing people is easier said than done.

The materialism of the wreckers disgusted Thoreau. Fortunately, he also had the opportunity to interview first mate Bangs as well as some of the other survivors. It seemed that most of those who survived had used planks from the ship to float to the shore of Fire Island.

The Elizabeth

Before it was time to return to Concord, Henry David Thoreau tore a button from a jacket that belonged to Giovanni Ossoli. Although, Giovanni's body was never found, his jacket washed to shore. Thoreau kept this button to remind himself of the fragility of life.

When Thoreau returned to Concord, he reported to Emerson what he had learned on Fire Island. Emerson listened intently and said, "So, you think that several brave men, with the help of a lifeboat, could have rescued the eight people who drowned on The Elizabeth?"

Thoreau replied, "I know the storm was fierce, but there was no need for loss of life. It also would have helped if the lifeboat was brought to shore sooner. Maybe it was impossible to rescue the passengers and crew, but at least an attempt should have been made. Unfortunately, though, the wreckers were more interested in plundering the cargo than they were in saving people's lives."

CHAPTER 11
MEMOIRS

Many people in America and Europe were shocked by the death of Margaret Ossoli. They wondered how someone so young could die so tragically. Those who had personally known Margaret were especially upset. They knew they had lost a dear friend.

Of course, Margaret's mother was heartbroken that she would never get to meet her grandson. All she could do was cry when she realized all that was left of Angelo was his lifeless body. Mrs. Fuller was robbed of her grandson and her daughter in a single day.

Back in Europe, Robert Browning was sad to be proven right about telling Margaret she should not sail on The Elizabeth. Margaret had not only been a great friend, but she had truly appreciated his poetry. And Angelo, of course, was such a happy toddler and had been friends with his son Pen.

Browning's wife, Elizabeth Barrett Browning, wasn't as troubled by Margaret's death as her husband. By nature, she was more aloof. Also, Elizabeth disagreed politically with Margaret, which prevented her from feeling much sorrow for Margaret's death.

The Elizabeth

Horace Sumner was another well-known person on The Elizabeth who perished. His older brother, Charles Sumner, was shocked to learn that his brother had drowned. Charles loved Horace and he had hoped his brother would be able to help him with his Senate campaign.

However, even without Horace, Charles became a United States Senator from Massachusetts. Charles was elected as a member of the Free Soil Party. It wasn't an easy election, but with Sumner's gift for oratory, he managed to pull off an upset victory against his Whig competitor.

Charles wished his brother Horace was still alive so they could celebrate his victory together. Unfortunately, though, his brother had drowned off the coast of Fire Island. At that moment, Charles Sumner decided he would take his position in the Senate seriously in order to honor his brother.

Margaret Ossoli, though, was the passenger with whom most people in America were familiar. She was the person they wanted to learn more about. So Ralph Waldo Emerson decided to write a book about Margaret. He collaborated with two other writers to explain important information about her life to the public.

An obituary in the newspaper would not satisfy the curiosity of the public when it came to someone who had accomplished the things Margaret had. Besides, Margaret had been Emerson's close friend. Surely, she deserved a book that he would co-author.

The other two writers of the Memoirs of Margaret Fuller Ossoli, were James Freeman Clarke and William Henry Channing. Each writer would write a memoir about Margaret. This meant there would be three memoirs in this book. All three writers worked diligently on this book, because they wanted to finish it in a timely manner.

It certainly would have been better had one of the authors been a woman, but they were doing their best to honor Margaret. Emerson felt good about having Clarke and Channing helping him write about Margaret. Clarke had been a close friend of Margaret's, and was the same age as her.

James Freeman Clarke had helped Margaret get some of her articles published, and was also a graduate of Harvard Divinity School. Of course, Emerson had graduated from that school as well. Clarke had radical religious beliefs which endeared him to Emerson. In fact, many church ladies had been shocked by the sermons Clarke preached. Emerson was certain that Margaret would approve of Clarke being a co-author of her memoirs.

William Henry Channing was an interesting fellow, as well. He was born in 1810 as was Margaret and James Freeman Clarke. Channing was a strong supporter of Women's Rights, and like Emerson and Clarke, was a graduate of Harvard Divinity School.

Channing's uncle, William Ellery Channing, had been the most famous Unitarian preacher in America. Although

The Elizabeth

Channing's uncle died in 1842, his spiritual influence was still felt in America. Indeed, William Ellery Channing had been like a father to his nephew. This was only natural since William Henry Channing lost his father in 1810, so tragically, Channing never knew him. Though Channing was close to his uncle, he was much more progressive than his uncle had ever been.

So these three men, who had all been Margaret's close friends, continued to work on her memoirs. Then, in 1852, the Memoirs of Margaret Fuller Ossoli was printed. The Memoirs was a two-volume book. Emerson, Clarke and Channing, though, wondered how the public would receive their book.

The response to the Memoirs was more impressive than they could have imagined. On the first day their book was available, it sold 1,000 copies. The public loved this book and it continued to sell quite well. In fact, the Memoirs of Margaret Fuller Ossoli sold so well that they had to keep publishing new editions.

Although the Memoirs wasn't a perfectly written book, it was a serious book about an important person. The Memoirs also helped people try to make sense of the terrible shipwreck that took place off the coast of Fire island. Anyone who read this book certainly had to consider the fragility of life.

Margaret's brother Arthur, who was ten years younger than her, respected his sister for supervising his education, especially since at that time women were not allowed to attend college. She was never allowed to go to Harvard, but she taught him so much that he was fully prepared to attend that college. Arthur Buckminster Fuller not only graduated from Harvard, but he also attended Harvard Divinity School. After finishing his studies, Arthur became a Unitarian Pastor.

Now, Arthur felt it was his turn to honor Margaret's memory. He decided to collect some of her writings and publish them as a book. The book Arthur edited was titled: *At Home and Abroad*. This book became available to the public in 1856. The writings collected in this book were about his sister's travels.

At Home and Abroad was an important book because it covered Margaret's experiences in the Great Lakes region as well as her European travels. Those who read this book could tell from the preface the great love that Arthur had for his sister.

Although Margaret did quite a bit of traveling during her life, she would have traveled even more if circumstances had permitted. *At Home and Abroad* gave readers the opportunity to accompany Margaret Ossoli on her adventures.

Unfortunately, 1856 wasn't a happy year for Arthur since his wife died from cholera. Now Arthur was a widower with two children to raise by himself. The only thing that comforted Arthur through the tragedy of losing his wife was his Christian beliefs.

Then, in 1859, Arthur published another collection of Margaret's writings. This book was titled: *Life Without and Life Within.* This new book was a collection of reviews, poems and other writings from Margaret Ossoli. Arthur now felt that he had truly honored his dear sister's memory.

Sadly, 1859 was also the year that Margaret and Arthur's mother died. Mrs. Fuller was 70 years old, which was considered a long life in those days. However, 1859 was also the year that Arthur remarried. Although Arthur wasn't as famous as his sister, he, too, was a remarkable person.

For instance, Arthur Buckminster Fuller preached his sermons without notes. Not many preachers had the ability or confidence to preach their sermons strictly from memory. Also, Arthur preached sermons that not only appealed to Unitarians, but also to people from other Christian denominations.

When Arthur was a student at Harvard, financing his education was difficult. He was compelled to work in order to raise the money to complete his studies. It was a few years after graduating from Harvard before he was able to attend Harvard Divinity School.

The fact that Arthur was able to graduate from Harvard Divinity School, despite financial hardship, was an example of his ability to overcome challenging obstacles. However, Arthur didn't know that a war was looming on the horizon. This war was the Civil War, a war that would tear the American nation apart.

CHAPTER 12
THE SECRET SIX

In 1852, the same year the *Memoirs of Margaret Fuller Ossoli* was published, *Uncle Tom's Cabin*, by Harriet Beecher Stowe, was also published. This novel clearly showed Stowe's opposition to slavery. She was an abolitionist from Connecticut who wanted to end slavery. Similar to Margaret Ossoli, she was a woman with strong convictions.

People who were opposed to slavery loved this book. Stowe's book not only sold well in America, but also in England. Indeed, the only book that was selling more copies was the Bible.

Due to various influences such as *Uncle Tom's Cabin*, the political environment in America was rapidly changing. The abolitionists were becoming more vocal in their beliefs and this was frightening to slave-owners in the Southern States. Even many people in the South who didn't own slaves were in favor of slavery. Clearly, America was becoming a divided country.

One of the greatest opponents of slavery, though, was Charles Sumner. Senator Sumner of Massachusetts was a brilliant orator, and he was also someone who hated slavery. Since Sumner was opposed to slavery, he wasn't willing to play nice with the southern Senators.

The Elizabeth

The Southerners in the Senate despised Sumner. He was threatening their way of life and they could not tolerate him. Finally, in 1856 things got so bad that Sumner was physically attacked on the floor of the Senate. His attacker was Preston Brooks, a Congressman from South Carolina.

Brooks nearly beat Sumner to death with a cane. When some Senators tried to defend Sumner, Congressman Keitt pointed a pistol at them. Keitt was a bad man himself, since he was the one who told Brooks to attack Sumner with a cane.

The violence happened because Sumner said bad things about a southern Senator in a speech. This southern Senator, though, happened to be Brooks' relative. Even though Sumner gave that speech two days before the beating, Brooks was still upset about the things Sumner had said.

Originally, Brooks planned to challenge Sumner to a duel. However, his friend Keitt convinced Brooks that Sumner wasn't worthy of a duel. So instead, Brooks brutally attacked Sumner with a cane on the floor of the Senate.

Many people in the South were happy about what Brooks had done. They even named a city and a county after him. However, the people in the northern states couldn't believe that Preston Brooks had gotten away with such barbaric actions. Indeed, a million copies of Charles Sumner's speech were published, since everyone wanted to know exactly what Sumner had said.

Sadly, Charles Sumner was injured so badly that it took him three years to recover from his injuries. During those years, the political leaders of Massachusetts refused to allow anyone to fill his Senate seat. They did this to serve as a reminder that the South had been cruel to their Senator.

Finally, in 1859, Sumner returned to the Senate. During his absence, the hostility between the northern states and southern states had increased. After Sumner was caned, an abolitionist named John Brown decided to use violence against anyone in Kansas who supported slavery.

Brown killed several people and felt that what he did was right. However, Brown had even bigger plans. He planned on taking over a Federal Armory in Harper's Ferry, Virginia. Taking over the armory would be the first step in his elaborate plan to free the slaves in the South.

John Brown knew it would be difficult to free the slaves. He also knew he needed to raise a lot of money before his dream could become a reality. So Brown found six influential men to help finance his efforts to free the slaves.

These men were the Secret Six. Only two of them were actually wealthy, but all of them hated slavery. So with their assistance, Brown was ready to implement the first stage of his plan. He had rifles and pikes as well as an army of 21 men. Several of the soldiers in John Brown's army were black men. He hoped to recruit more black men into his army, so he could fight a guerrilla war in the southern states. He stormed the Armory at Harper's Ferry and successfully captured it.

John Brown also captured some of the men who lived in the area and held them as hostages. Some of Brown's sons were also part of his small army. Unfortunately, Brown's plans fell apart when a military force led by Robert E. Lee surrounded him.

Lee and his soldiers killed ten of Brown's men and wounded others. John Brown was severely wounded before being taken prisoner. Some of Brown's men escaped and were later captured, but some of his soldiers escaped and were never captured. Since Brown wasn't successful in accomplishing his mission, he knew it was only a matter of time before he was executed.

Slave-owners in the South would never allow someone like Brown to live. Indeed, it was a miracle that he had survived the wounds he received. He might be given a sham trial, but that was the most he could hope for.

What really upset the southern slave owners, though, was the Secret Six. Documents were discovered that linked these six influential men to John Brown. The names of these men were: Thomas Wentworth Higginson, Samuel Gridley Howe, Theodore Parker, Franklin Benjamin Sanborn, Gerrit Smith and George Luther Stearns.

Now the members of the Secret Six were under intense government scrutiny. Each of these men needed to decide the best way to react to the possibility of being arrested. Theodore Parker's decision was the easiest, since he was on vacation in Italy. Indeed, Parker was suffering from tuberculosis and hoping to make a recovery when he learned about Brown's failed attempt to free the slaves. Since it was unlikely that he would be returned to America, the only danger he faced now, was poor health.

Then, in November of 1859, Theodore Parker learned that John Brown was going to be executed. Parker knew there was nothing he could do to save his friend's life. However, Parker did write a letter that was titled: John Brown's Expedition. This was a lengthy letter that explained why John Brown's actions were justified.

This letter was written in 1859 and published in 1860. Although Parker was dying from tuberculosis, he refused to waver in his support for John Brown. Even though he was a Unitarian minister, Theodore Parker believed that violence was acceptable if it would free the slaves. In May of 1860, Parker died from tuberculosis in Florence, Italy at the age of 49.

Back in America, though, the remaining members of the Secret Six were in danger of being arrested. Indeed, Franklin Benjamin Sanborn was arrested by five Federal Marshals on April 3, 1860. The marshals even took Sanborn from his home in handcuffs.

Under ordinary circumstances, Sanborn would have been forced to testify about his involvement with John Brown. However, Sanborn's friends and neighbors in Concord, Massachusetts, wouldn't allow the marshals to take him away. They were angry with the marshals and they prevented law enforcement from kidnapping their friend.

The Elizabeth

Sanborn never had to testify, because an important judge in Massachusetts ruled that he didn't need to. Most of the remaining members of the Secret Six, though, were quite nervous about being arrested. However, there was one member of the Secret Six who was fearless.

Thomas Wentworth Higginson was proud of what he had done. He even put together a plan to prevent John Brown from being executed. Nobody ever carried out the plan, though, since it was too risky. Higginson dared law enforcement to arrest him, but they never did.

Higginson was also a graduate of Harvard Divinity School. There was something about Harvard Divinity School that produced radical thinkers. Higginson was definitely someone who would never pretend that he hadn't supported John Brown.

Each member of the Secret Six reacted differently to the possibility of being arrested. The fact that the Secret Six were never punished, infuriated southern slave-owners. However, many people in the northern states approved of their actions.

CHAPTER 13
WAR

Henry David Thoreau, who had been Margaret Ossoli's friend, defended the actions of John Brown. Although he wasn't a member of the Secret Six, Thoreau gave speeches to explain that Brown wasn't crazy. Indeed, Thoreau thought Brown was a great man.

After Brown was executed, Thoreau's speech was included in a book titled: *Echoes of Harper's Ferry*. Though Thoreau was in poor health, he still had the strength to speak up for what he thought was right. Indeed, it was impossible for the opinionated Thoreau to do otherwise.

On, November 6, 1860, Abraham Lincoln was elected President of the United States. He was unacceptable to the people who lived in the South. There was even a plot to assassinate him before he could take office on March 4, 1861.

Although Southerners were frightened of Lincoln because he was opposed to slavery, Charles Sumner thought Lincoln was too moderate on this issue. Despite being nearly beaten to death in 1856, Sumner would never compromise on the issue of slavery.

Sumner was now a member of the Republican Party and Abraham Lincoln was the first Republican President. However, the southern states were in the process of succeeding from the Union. Then on April 12, 1861, the South attacked Fort Sumter in South Carolina.

Now, America was at war with itself. Since, Lincoln wasn't willing to allow the Confederates to succeed from the Union, war was the only option. Events were moving at a rapid pace, and Lincoln hoped he could prevent America from becoming two countries.

When the Civil War began, Arthur Buckminster Fuller joined the Union Army. Because of his religious training, he served as a chaplain for the North. In the military, though, Margaret Ossoli's brother wouldn't just be preaching to Unitarians.

Arthur was forced to become more tolerant when he began working with soldiers whose religious beliefs were different from his. Arthur became good friends with the men serving in the Union Army, and he did his best to help his fellow soldiers.

Some military chaplains tried to avoid danger, but Fuller stayed on the battlefield and tried to help the wounded. Since Fuller was opposed to slavery, he was proud to serve in the Union Army.

On, March 9, 1862, Arthur witnessed an event that fascinated him. This event was a naval battle between the

Ironclads. The North had a naval blockade on the South, which the Confederacy desperately wanted to disrupt. So the Confederates built an Ironclad warship they called the Merrimack.

The Merrimack was a new type of ship, and initially it had some success in breaking the Northern blockade. The North, though, had an answer to the Merrimack. They had built their own Ironclad called the Monitor. The Monitor confronted the Merrimack and they battled for hours.

Neither battleship could gain an advantage, so the ironclads stopped fighting each other. Arthur was happy that the Union battleship performed so well. He also knew that he was witnessing a new type of warfare. Fuller hoped the war would end soon and that the North would be victorious.

Back in Concord, Massachusetts, Henry David Thoreau was dying from tuberculosis. His family and friends wanted to help him, but there was nothing they could do. Margaret Ossoli's old friend Jameson Fisher visited Thoreau. Tears filled Fisher's eyes, when he realized Thoreau was going to die.

A few days later, on April 12, 1862, Thoreau died. This great man was only 44 years old, but tuberculosis was an incurable disease in those days. Thoreau had been a true friend to Margaret. Even when many others turned against her, Thoreau always admired Margaret.

The Elizabeth

The cause, though, that had really been important to Margaret, was Italian Independence. In 1861, Giuseppe Garibaldi was once again fighting to unify Italy. He hated Pope Pius IX even more than Margaret had and Garibaldi wasn't going to rest until he captured Rome.

When Garibaldi remembered how the Pope had destroyed the Roman Republic in 1849, his blood still boiled. Although, Garibaldi was quite busy fighting in Italy, he was still interested in what was happening in the American Civil War.

Garibaldi thought highly of President Lincoln and hoped that the North would win the Civil War. The North offered Garibaldi the rank of Major General if he would help the Union Army in America. Garibaldi politely declined, but he always publicly supported Lincoln.

In America, when Union soldiers were marching, they liked to sing songs. John Brown's Body was a song they often sang. However, Julia Ward Howe changed the words to this song. The new version was called the "Battle Hymn of the Republic". She wrote the lyrics to this song in a single morning.

Howe's husband was Samuel Gridley Howe. He was much older than her, and also a member of the Secret Six. Their family was initially placed under intense scrutiny when John Brown was captured. Now that the South had seceded from the Union, Howe's husband was no longer in danger of being arrested.

On December 10, 1862, Arthur Buckminster Fuller was discharged from the military. Although he had served bravely, his health was too frail for him to continue. While Fuller was preparing to return home, preparations were underway for the Battle of Fredericksburg.

Instead of returning home, Fuller decided to take part in the battle. On the first day of the battle, December 11, Fuller was killed. He died at the age of 40. His sister, Margaret Ossoli had also died at the age of 40. Many people attended Arthur Buckminster Fuller's funeral, which was held in Boston.

Fuller's younger brother, Richard Frederick Fuller, decided he would write a book about Arthur titled: *Chaplain Fuller*. Although it was a lengthy book, it was ready for publication in 1863. This was also the year of the Emancipation Proclamation.

Thomas Wentworth Higginson, a member of the Secret Six, fought in the Civil War. Higginson was a Unitarian Minister willing to fight against slavery. He started out as a Captain in 1862 and eventually became a Colonel. In 1864, Higginson was wounded and could no longer serve in the military.

The Civil War was longer and killed more soldiers than most people could have imagined. However, in 1865, the Union Army clearly had the upper hand. On, April 9, Robert E. Lee surrendered in Virginia. Some other Confederate Generals held out for a bit longer, but the Civil War was essentially over.

The Elizabeth

However, on April 14, Abraham Lincoln was shot, and he died the next morning. Now, Andrew Johnson was the President. He wasn't the President that many in the North wanted, but he was the one they were stuck with.

The first thing President Johnson wanted to do was execute anyone who had been part of the plot to assassinate Lincoln. Johnson refused to show mercy to anyone who had helped to assassinate Abraham Lincoln.

One of the reasons Andrew Johnson dealt harshly with the conspirators was because they had also planned to kill him. However, the person who was supposed to kill Johnson lost his nerve, so Johnson's life was spared.

Johnson also had no intention of being lenient with the leaders of the Confederacy. Jefferson Davis, the President of the Confederacy, was captured on May 10 and put in prison on May 19. The South had been defeated and Johnson had no sympathy for people he viewed as traitors.

In Massachusetts, some of Margaret's Ossoli's old friends and acquaintances were still trying to make sense of the war that had just been fought. Nathaniel Hawthorne, though, who had once been Margaret's friend, had died in 1864. However, other friends such as Ralph Waldo Emerson were still alive.

Amos Bronson Alcott, who had given Margaret her first paid teaching job, was still just as energetic as ever. His daughter, Louisa May Alcott had served as a nurse for several weeks during the Civil War. However, when she contracted typhoid, she was no longer able to help the Union soldiers.

Amos was proud of his daughter for helping with the war effort. He was also happy that his daughter Louisa was interested in becoming a writer. Although the Civil War caused much suffering, people did their best to continue living despite their grief.

CHAPTER 14
HORACE GREELEY

Margaret Ossoli's friend Horace Greeley had been terribly upset when she drowned in 1850. He had been her former employer at the *New York Tribune* and Ossoli had even lived in his home for a few years. Despite, Greeley's grief over Margaret's death, he still had many responsibilities that kept him very busy.

For instance, he was still the publisher of the *New York Tribune*. Also, Greeley enjoyed dabbling in politics. Indeed, Horace Greeley had an opinion on just about everything. After the Civil War ended, Greeley found a new cause to support. Greeley thought it was unjust that Jefferson Davis was being kept in jail.

Although, Greeley was from the North, he felt that President Johnson was treating Davis unfairly. Davis was being held as a prisoner at Fort Monroe in Virginia. Greeley believed Davis should either have a trial or that the former Confederate President should be released from jail.

So, in 1867, Horace Greeley, Gerrit Smith and Cornelius Vanderbilt, paid the large bond that was required to free Jefferson Davis. Because of this, many people in the North were angry with Greeley. They didn't think it was right for

The Elizabeth

him to help a man who had caused so much turmoil in America.

Some people even canceled their subscriptions to the *New York Tribune*. However, Greeley was a clever businessman so he was able to weather the storm. Indeed, it wasn't long before people once again wanted to read Greeley's newspaper, in order to learn about the Presidential Election.

In 1868, Ulysses S. Grant was elected President. The election was closer than many people believed it would be. Surprisingly, Grant even managed to lose in New York. This was embarrassing for Horace Greeley, since he had used his newspaper to attack Grant's opponent.

Horatio Seymour, the candidate for the Democrats, had received almost as many votes as Ulysses S. Grant. However, Grant received many more electoral votes. Although Grant had been a talented General, it remained to be seen if he would be a good President.

Though Greeley was best known as the publisher of the *New York Tribune*, he was also a bit of a dreamer. In 1869, he became interested in creating a Utopian colony in the Colorado Territory. In fact, today, Horace Greeley would be talking to Nathan Meeker about this topic.

After inviting Nathan into his home, Greeley said, "Nathan, you have done great work for me at the Tribune. However, I want to hear about your trip to the Colorado Territory. Do you think it's possible to start a Utopian community in the Colorado Territory?"

Meeker replied, "I found the perfect location, but in order for this community to be successful, we will need to find people of good character. The success of this community will depend entirely on the hard work and self-discipline of the people who are willing to take part in this experiment."

Greeley responded, "I couldn't agree more. We don't want any drunkards or money-grubbers destroying the morale of our town. Do you think there is potential for farming in the area you selected?" Meeker said, "Yes, but I would recommend using modern irrigation techniques."

Then Greeley told Meeker, "I will supply the money necessary to make this Utopian community a reality. Unfortunately, I won't be able to live there since I have responsibilities here in New York City. Are you willing to move to the Colorado Territory and organize this town for me?" Meeker responded, "Yes," and the two men shook hands.

Although Greeley was a successful businessman, he was also an idealist. It broke his heart when he thought about how many soldiers were killed during the Civil War. Greeley, though, hoped his new Utopian community would show others a better way to live.

Meanwhile, over in Italy, Giuseppe Garibaldi was still trying to get his revenge on Pope Pius IX. Every time Garibaldi came close to capturing Rome, though, French soldiers stopped him. However, in 1870, the French got in a war with the Prussians.

Since the French were fighting the Prussians, they needed all their available soldiers. So Napoleon III withdrew his troops from Rome. Now the Pope was no longer protected, and it wouldn't take long for someone to take advantage of his weakened position.

Victor Emmanuel II was the person who captured Rome. As the King of Italy, he was able to send the Italian Army to Rome. Even though the French Garrison had left Rome, Pope Pius IX still had some soldiers. However, he knew he could not withstand the might of the Italian Army.

The Pope's soldiers put up very little resistance to the Italian Army. So, very quickly, the Pope lost control of Rome. The Pope was bitter and angry with Victor Emmanuel II. To be honest, though, the King really didn't care what the Pope thought. The King of Italy had succeeded in unifying his Country. Now Italy would no longer be dominated by foreign countries.

This was something for which Margaret Ossoli and many others had sacrificed everything. Finally, Italy would be governed by Italians instead of by Austria and France. Also, Margaret and Garibaldi had their revenge, since the Pope no longer ruled Rome or the Papal States. The only thing Garibaldi regretted was not being able to take part in capturing Rome.

Back in America, Horace Greeley had decided to run for President. This seemed like an odd decision, since Greeley wasn't much of a politician. Indeed, he had tried to get elected to Congress many times. Usually, though, Greeley lost when he ran for office.

However, Greeley was unhappy with the job Ulysses S. Grant was doing. Greeley felt Grant was corrupt and that he no longer deserved to be President. So Greeley attended the Liberal Republican Party Convention. He was planning to compete at the Convention as a candidate for President.

It wouldn't be easy, though, for Greeley to win his party's nomination. He knew there would be other strong candidates such as Charles Francis Adams and Lyman Trumbull. Adams was the son of former President, John Quincy Adams, and Trumbull was an Illinois Senator.

After the first ballot, it looked like Adams would probably be the party's nominee. However, somehow Greeley won his party's nomination on the sixth ballot. Now, Horace Greeley would be running for President against Ulysses S. Grant.

When the Democrats held their Convention, they also decided to support Horace Greeley. Greeley was pleased with this, because it meant that he would have two political parties helping him. Initially, it seemed like Greeley had a good chance of becoming President.

Grant, though, was supported by many wealthy businessmen. Also, Greeley's wife became sick while he was campaigning. In fact, she became so sick that Greeley stopped campaigning. Tragically, several days before the Presidential Election, Greeley's wife died.

The Elizabeth

When the votes were counted, it was obvious that Ulysses S. Grant was going to be re-elected. Losing his wife and the election was too much to bear for Greeley. He was no longer able to keep it together and he suffered a nervous breakdown. Horace Greeley was sent to the Choate House sanitarium.

After staying a few weeks at the sanitarium, Greeley died on November 29, 1872, at the age of 61. Margaret Ossoli had greatly admired Greeley and so had many others. Many of the people who had been bad to Greeley during the Presidential Election, though, wanted to honor him after he was dead.

Horace Greeley's funeral was held at the Church of The Divine Paternity, a church he would have approved of since he attended services there. Greeley was buried in Brooklyn. He had done what he could to help his country, but now others would need to do their part.

Charles Sumner, though, was still a Senator from Massachusetts. He had supported Greeley during the Election of 1872 because he also believed Ulysses S. Grant was a corrupt President. Unfortunately, though, Grant was re-elected.

Sumner was lucky to be alive after the beating he received from Preston Brooks in 1856. He was still a talented public speaker and, even though his beliefs were sometimes controversial, he continued to work on the issues he believed in.

Even in Massachusetts, there were many people who didn't always agree with him. Sadly, Charles Sumner died on

March 11, 1874, at the age of 63. Similar to Greeley, Sumner received greater respect after his death. Truly, America had lost two great men in a short period of time.

CHAPTER 15
JULIA WARD HOWE

Julia Ward Howe was born on May 27, 1819, in New York City. Her father was an influential banker and her mother was a poet. Sadly, her mother died when Julia was only five years old. Since Julia's father was wealthy, she received a good education, which was unusual for girls in those days.

Because of her privileged upbringing, she had the opportunity to meet many famous people. Julia's father, though, died when she was twenty years old. Her father had raised her with very strict religious beliefs. Julia, though, decided she wanted to become a Unitarian. The Unitarian religion was more progressive than the Episcopalian faith in which Julia had been raised.

Julia married Samuel Gridley Howe. Samuel was a bit of a macho man who was much older than she was. In his younger years, Samuel traveled to Greece to fight in the Greek Revolution. Since he was a graduate of Harvard Medical School, he was also able to care for the wounded.

After several years of fighting, Samuel traveled to Paris. While he was living in Paris, Samuel became involved in the July Revolution. Samuel was now both a doctor and a revolutionary. He decided, though, that he had done enough fighting, so he returned to America.

The Elizabeth

When Julia met Samuel, he was working at a school that helped blind people. He was a very talented man who wanted to help others. Julia was very impressed with Samuel and they decided to get married on April 23, 1843. Although, they loved each other, they had many disagreements.

Julia was a feminist, while Samuel believed that a woman should stay home and raise the children. Since they were both stubborn, it was surprising that they stayed together. Somehow, they did, though, and they both became committed to many of the same causes.

One person Julia really admired was Margaret Ossoli. Julia even had the opportunity to listen to Margaret speak. Of course, in those days, she was known as Margaret Fuller. Julia thought to herself, "I want to fight for Women's Rights the way Margaret does."

When, Margaret Ossoli died in 1850, Julia Ward Howe felt like she had lost a friend. Even though she had never been close friends with Margaret, Julia had been influenced by her. "Someday," Julia thought, "I will write a book about Margaret Ossoli."

One thing Julia and her husband agreed upon was that they hated slavery. Indeed, Samuel was an important abolitionist. Since he had fought in European Revolutions, Samuel Gridley Howe wasn't opposed to using violence to accomplish his goals.

In 1859, though, it was discovered that Samuel had been a member of the Secret Six. The Secret Six was a group of six influential men who had financed John Brown's raid on a Federal Armory. When the militant abolitionist Brown was captured, documents were found that showed Samuel had helped him financially.

Since Samuel didn't want to be prosecuted, he briefly moved to Canada. Although Julia was against slavery, she didn't approve of her husband's way of doing things. Samuel, though, controlled her money, so he was able to keep secrets from his wife.

Soon the Civil War started, and during the war, Julia wrote the words to the "Battle Hymn of The Republic". She thought of the lyrics when she was having trouble sleeping. Julia knew that if she went back to bed, she would forget the words floating around in her head. So she got out of bed and found a pencil to write the verses to the "Battle Hymn of The Republic".

Similar to Margaret Ossoli, Julia loved learning new things. Philosophy intrigued her, and she was also fluent in several languages. It wasn't easy raising several children and also being a scholar. Although Samuel didn't want Julia to better herself, she did it anyway.

After the Civil War Julia became a pacifist, and also believed that women should have the right to vote. Since Samuel was tired of arguing with his wife, he let her do what she wanted to do. So Julia became more involved in various activities.

The Elizabeth

For instance, in 1868, Julia Ward Howe was one of the women who founded the New England Women's Club. This was an intellectual club created for women. Men could also become members, so Ralph Waldo Emerson decided to join.

The organization, though, that meant the most to Julia, was the New England Woman Suffrage Association. This organization was a group of women who believed women should be allowed to vote. Julia was the first President of this organization.

Sadly, Julia's husband died on January 9, 1876 at the age of 74. He hadn't been a perfect man, but in many ways he was far ahead of his time. Samuel Gridley Howe had done his best to help the blind, fought in European Revolutions, and worked to end slavery.

Although Julia Ward Howe was sad that her husband died, she was pleased her children were doing well with their lives. Julia had six children, but the youngest had died during the Civil War while he was still a small child. Although Julia missed her son, she knew he had been taken to a better place.

Something else, though, was troubling Julia. For many years she had wanted to write a book about Margaret Ossoli. Although others had already written about Margaret, Julia also wanted to honor her memory. Julia wondered why she kept procrastinating on such an important task.

However, after Ralph Waldo Emerson died in 1882, Julia decided to begin writing her book about Margaret Ossoli. She started to do research about Margaret. The hardest part of the biography for Julia to write was when Margaret, Giovanni, Celeste and Angelo drowned. Julia wept when she thought about Margaret dying within sight of Fire Island.

Soon, Julia had finished writing: *Margaret Fuller*. Her book was published in 1883 and it reminded people about Margaret's accomplishments. Julia's book also made people remember a tragic shipwreck that had taken place in 1850. When The Elizabeth sank, many hearts were broken. Just then, Julia thought to herself, "Margaret Ossoli is too important to ever be forgotten."

The next year, in 1884, though, Julia's older brother Sam died. Julia and Sam had been very close their entire lives. At one time, Sam Ward had been married to one of the wealthiest ladies in America. However, sadly, his wife died only three years after they were married.

Julia had always been proud of Sam, because he was a progressive thinker. Their father had been so conservative that Julia had rebelled a bit when he died in 1839. That was also the same year Julia's brother Henry died.

"So many people I care about are no longer with me," Julia thought. Since her grief was too much to bear, Julia decided to visit her youngest daughter. Julia's daughter, Maud, was a famous socialite. Maud worried her mother, though, since she was 28 years old and had never been married.

The Elizabeth

Maud Howe entered her mother's home and said, "Mother, what's wrong." Maud had never seen her mother this upset before. This frightened her, because she was used to her mother being the rock everyone else relied on.

Julia replied, "You probably already know that your Uncle Sam died. However, his death has hit me very hard. My brother was five years older than me, and was always my favorite sibling. Even though he was 70 years old, I feel that someone very important has been taken from me."

Maud burst into tears, "Now you have made me emotional mother. I came over here to be strong for you, but I can see that I have failed." Julia responded by giving her daughter a hug. As both women continued to cry, Julia said, "You haven't failed. I needed your support and you gave it to me."

Julia's brother had died in Italy, but he was buried in New York City. Sam Ward was a man who had made and lost several fortunes. He was also the most talented lobbyist in the history of Washington DC. Although Julia missed her brother terribly, she knew there were still many things she needed to accomplish in her own life.

A few years later, in 1887, Julia learned that her daughter Maud was getting married. This warmed her heart. Maud was marrying an artist named John Elliott. Elliot was from England and he was four years younger than Maud. Soon Maud was married, but Julia didn't get to see her much.

This was because the young newlyweds were traveling all the time. Julia didn't get her feelings hurt, though, since she also had a passion for travel. Julia was impressed with Maud's husband and was amazed whenever she saw his paintings. Elliott had studied with the best artists in Europe, and now he was also a great artist.

However, her daughter Maud was more of a writer. Julia also had a nephew named Francis Marion Crawford who was already a famous novelist. Julia adored Crawford and she was happy for his success.

Something else that was important to Julia Ward Howe was religion. When she was a young woman, Julia had disagreed with the conservative religious beliefs of her father. In 1893, though, Julia had the opportunity to speak at an important religious event.

The speech she gave was titled: What is Religion? Julia traveled to Chicago for this event because she supported the progressive ideals of the World's Parliament of Religions.

CHAPTER 16
LEGACY

Although Julia Ward Howe had already written a book about Margaret Ossoli, she remained fascinated with her. One of the reasons Julia respected her, was because Margaret had fought for Women's Rights long before it was popular. Now, Julia found herself frequently turning to Margaret's writings for inspiration.

The more Julia thought about Margaret's influence on Women's Rights, the more she realized that more needed to be done to honor Margaret's accomplishments. So Julia decided that a special memorial pavilion should be created for Margaret. She helped raise the money necessary to build the pavilion on Fire Island in 1901.

Julia's daughters were proud of their mom for her desire to show respect for Margaret Ossoli. Julia's oldest daughter, though, who was also named Julia, had died in 1886. However, Florence, Laura and Maud were still very much alive. They were also proud of their mother because she believed that women should have the right to vote.

Florence, Laura and Maud had watched their mother fight enthusiastically for Women's Suffrage for many years. Julia's cause had become their cause, as well. However,

The Elizabeth

Julia knew it was unlikely that she would live long enough to actually be able to vote. She believed, though, that her daughters would have the right to vote.

Sometimes Julia wondered why men didn't want to allow women to vote. Her own husband, in fact, had never cared about Women's Rights. Julia, though, continued working and organizing for Women's Suffrage until her death at the age of 91, on October 17, 1910.

Since she had touched many lives, thousands of people attended Julia's memorial service. Of course, everyone sang the "Battle Hymn of the Republic" since Julia had written the words to that song. She was buried at the Mount Auburn Cemetery in Cambridge, Massachusetts.

This was the same cemetery where Margaret, Giovanni and Angelo had a special burial plot. Although Margaret and Giovanni's bodies were never found, they still had a monument built for them at the cemetery where their son Angelo was buried.

In New Zealand and Australia, women were already allowed to vote. However, in most parts of the world, they were still barred from voting. For women such as Margaret Ossoli and Julia Ward Howe, allowing women to vote was simply common sense. Common sense, though, was in short supply in those days.

Sadly, in 1913, Margaret's memorial pavilion was ruined by a storm. Then, in 1914, something even worse happened.

That was the year World War I began. What a horrible time that was. Although, America wasn't directly involved in the war, it seemed like only a matter of time before she would be.

When the war began, Julia's daughter Maud was very upset. So she told her husband, "John, we have left the men in charge of running this world, and now they are ruining it. Would it be so bad for women to vote, when all that we get from men is destruction and bloodshed?"

Her husband replied, "How can I disagree with you when what you say makes so much sense? Although, I don't believe that women can solve all the world's problems, I do believe they should be given the chance to try. I also know that your mother would be proud of the work you have done in the Women's Suffrage movement."

Maud responded, "My mother was the real champion for Women's Rights. In fact, my sisters and I are planning to write a book about her. I know that many people will want to read about mother since she was such an important woman."

So Maud and her sisters began writing a book about their mother. They worked quickly on the book, and it was published in 1916. Then in 1917, Maud, Florence and Laura won a Pulitzer Prize for their book. This was a great accomplishment for the three sisters, and they were happy to win such a prestigious award.

What, Maud really wanted though, was for World War I to end. Her eyes filled with tears when she thought about

The Elizabeth

American soldiers dying in Europe. What a senseless tragedy this war had been. There was a time, prior to the war, when Maud and her husband lived in Italy. Now, though, all there was in Europe was trench warfare and suffering.

Maud and her husband John were thankful when World War I ended in 1918. Although John Elliott was originally from England, he was glad to see the American soldiers returning home. However, his joy turned to grief when people began dying from the Spanish Flu.

The Spanish Flu was a terrible disease that was killing people all over the world. John and Maud were worried about the Spanish Flu, and hoped that a cure would be found. Sometimes Maud wondered why there had to be so much suffering in the world.

In 1918, the same year the war ended, women gained the right to vote in Germany and Poland. Also that year, women in England gained partial voting rights. Maud felt that this was encouraging news, so she redoubled her efforts to help women vote in America.

She thought to herself, "Soon women in America will be allowed to vote." Maud Howe Elliott's confidence was not misplaced, and American women voted in the Presidential Election of 1920. When Maud voted, she had to admit to herself that it felt pretty damn good.

Many Women's Rights hadn't yet been achieved, but this was definitely a step in the right direction. Maud wished her mother had lived to see this day. But she could feel her mother's presence when she cast her vote, so this experience meant a lot to Maud, even though her mother was only there in spirit.

For the most part, Maud was happy with her life. However, she was very upset when her sister Florence and brother Henry died in 1922. She felt a little better, though, when she realized that her siblings had already lived long lives. Maud's heart was broken again, though, when her husband died in 1925.

John Elliott meant the world to her, and they had an amazing life together. They lived in Chicago and Italy, but more recently they had been living in Newport, Rhode Island. Maud mourned the loss of her husband for a few days and she thought she would never stop crying.

However, eventually Maud was able to stop mourning. She thought to herself, "I am a very lucky woman to have been married to such a talented artist. John and I were happily married for many years, which is something many people never experience. Even my own mother had a very unhappy marriage. Instead of being sad, I am going to be grateful for the time I had with my husband."

Later on, though, Maud began thinking about The Elizabeth. Although, The Elizabeth was a cargo ship that had sunk five years before Maud was born, she often thought about the tragedy. How sad it had been that Margaret Ossoli and Horace Sumner drowned on that awful day in 1850.

The Elizabeth

Although many people had forgotten about Margaret, Maud certainly hadn't. She felt Margaret had been a great woman who was still worthy of respect. Maud was also proud of Margaret because she had recognized the importance of unifying Italy.

Sometimes, though, when Maud heard a strong and noisy storm, she was still fearful that a shipwreck would occur. Suddenly, Maud thought to herself, "Even in 1925 it is dangerous to travel on a ship."

THE END